marks noted on this page,
CB/ACR 1/19

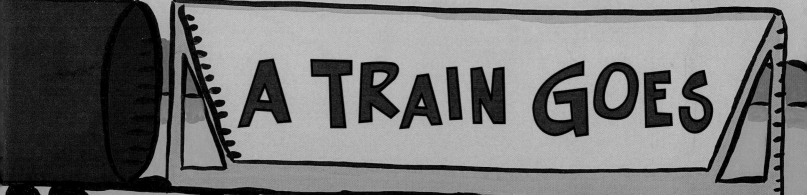

A TRAIN GOES

CLICKETY-CLACK

by Jonathan London
illustrated by Denis Roche

Henry Holt and Company ◆ New York

THIS BOOK BELONGS TO:
_____

Henry Holt and Company, LLC
Publishers since 1866
175 Fifth Avenue
New York, New York 10010
www.henryholtchildrensbooks.com

Henry Holt® is a registered trademark of Henry Holt and Company, LLC.
Text copyright © 2007 by Jonathan London
Illustrations copyright © 2007 by Denis Roche
All rights reserved. Distributed in Canada by H. B. Fenn and Company Ltd.

Library of Congress Cataloging-in-Publication Data
London, Jonathan.
A train goes clickety-clack / by Jonathan London; illustrated by Denis Roche.—1st ed.
p.   cm.
Summary: Easy-to-read, rhyming text describes the sounds of,
and uses for, different kinds of trains.
ISBN-13: 978-0-8050-7972-2 / ISBN-10: 0-8050-7972-6
[1. Railroad trains—Fiction. 2. Stories in rhyme.] I. Roche, Denis (Denis M.), ill. II. Title.
PZ8.3.L8433Tqd 2007   [E]—dc22   2006030765

First Edition—2007 / Designed by Véronique Lefèvre Sweet
The artist used gouache on paper to create the illustrations for this book.
Printed in the United States of America on acid-free paper. ∞

1 3 5 7 9 10 8 6 4 2

For Helene and Gerardo, and for
train lovers young and old
—J. L.

For Henry, with love
—D. R.

A train could be old.

A train could be new.

A train could have one engine

or a train could have two.

A train could be fast,
like a silvery gleam.

Or a train could be slow,

like a lazy stream.

A train goes *chugga-chugga*.
A train goes *clickety-clack*.

A train goes *jiggly-rumba*
on down that long track.

A train hauls cattle.

A train hauls steel.

A train carries people

who sit for a meal.

A train's wheels clatter.

A train's couplings clang.

A train's boiler hisses.

A train's bumpers bang.

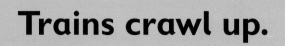

Trains crawl up.

Trains ROOAAAAR down.

Trains blow whistles—

CHOO-CHOOOOOOOO—

and rumble through town.

If I were an engineer,
I could make the train go.

Or I could swing a red lantern

and watch the night glow.

Jonathan London is the author of *A Truck Goes Rattley-Bumpa* and more than eighty books for young readers, including *Wiggle Waggle* and the ever-popular Froggy books. He lives with his family in Graton, California.

Denis Roche is a former schoolteacher and the illustrator of *A Truck Goes Rattley-Bumpa*. She has written and illustrated many books for young readers, including *Best Class Picture Ever!* and *Little Pig Is Capable*. She lives with her family in Providence, Rhode Island.